Für Matteo

Supported by

ARTS COUNCIL ENGLAND

© 2005 Beltz & Gelberg
in der Verlagsgruppe Beltz · Weinheim Basel
Wingedchariot Press 2006

Wingedchariot Design by Grafin
Printed in Portugal by Ambar

www.wingedchariot.com

When We Lived in Uncle's Hat

Peter Stamm · Jutta Bauer

Translated by
Nani Schumman and Kate Connolly

WingedChariot Press

The house with the blue light

When we lived in the house with the blue light, the sun was so hot we had to keep the curtains closed. All day long we heard the music from the dance school upstairs and on some days in spring we could smell lilac outside. The blue light was always on and when we went to bed we left the doors open so we could see it. When it rained we heard water gushing down the pipes, and the drops dripping onto the pavement from the leaves of the tulip tree.

Father read four newspapers, Mother bought three chairs.
Grandma knitted two pairs of striped socks for each of us and Grandpa lost his sunglasses.
But my sister was always sad.
So … we moved to the bus.

The bus

When we lived on the bus we paid no rent, but we had to punch a new
ticket every hour. We met lots of people, but they all looked so serious
and were always too busy to talk. Sometimes we hid under the seats
and listened to the engine roaring like a lion. Sometimes we'd press the
"stop" button, even though we didn't want to get off. The whole day
smelt of petrol and sweat and we saw the same streets over and over
again. We could only read at the railway station when the bus stopped
for a few minutes to wait for the trains or simply for the hands of the
clock to move.

Mother learnt four languages.
Grandpa lost three teeth.
My brother made two new friends and Grandma got pneumonia.
But Father fell out with Mother.
So … we moved to the forest.

The forest

When we lived in the forest we learnt the names of all the mushrooms and mosses and ferns. During the week we were woken at 6.30 by the roar of the chainsaws and on Sundays the woodpecker woke us at 8.30. Some nights we climbed the highest tree to gaze at the city and watch the red light of the radio tower on the hill blink in the darkness.
We built ourselves a tree house because the ground was often damp.
We gave up going to school and instead we collected nuts and sold them to the squirrels. Then we would go into town to spend our earnings on high-heeled shoes.

Father had his 40th birthday.
Grandma brushed her teeth three times a day.
Grandpa said everything twice and my sister kissed a boy for the first time.
But Mother lost the last of her books.
So ... we moved to the church roof.

The church roof

When we lived on the church roof we had to get up very early on
Sundays and we didn't go to bed before the clock struck midnight.
We always knew what the time was. In the summer, long after the sun
had set, the roof tiles were still warm. When we played football, the
ball rolled off the roof. So we would gaze at the passing clouds and
make up endless stories. We had a kitchen and a living room and each
of us had our own bedroom, even though there were no walls in
between.

My brother found four coins in the collection box.
Grandma said three times that they didn't belong to him.
Mother twice went missing, and Father made one promise.
But Grandpa was sad every time they buried someone in the cemetery
down below.
So ... we moved to Aunty's violin.

Aunty's violin

When we lived in Aunty's violin, the floor creaked with every step. When Aunty played Gypsy songs the furniture fell over. Mother hung the washing on the violin string, and Father shouted: "earplugs!" The violin smelt of wood and resin and old varnish. When the violin was in its case it was dark and stuffy and we couldn't get out. But when Aunty practised, it was light, and we would sometimes sing along. Then we all felt good.

Grandpa knew the names of all four strings.
My sister learnt three songs by heart.
Father bought himself two pairs of earplugs and Mother baked one chocolate cake.
But Aunty gave up the violin.
So … we moved to a hotel.

The hotel

When we lived in the hotel we got fresh towels every day and little
pieces of soap, which smelled of roses. My parents drank wine with
every meal and on Sundays we had pudding. When we got home from
school we had to ask for the key at Reception. We took the lift to
the upper floors and knocked on the doors before running away.
At night we heard a loud knocking from the heating pipes and through
the blinds we saw the glow of the neon signs outside.

We heard strange sounds coming from Room 4.
On the third floor there was a woman with a small dog.
Every evening there were always two pairs of dirty shoes outside the
room next door, except for once when there was only one pair.
But my brother ate one of the soaps and got ill.
So ... we moved to nowhere.

Nowhere

When we lived nowhere we had to pick up our letters from the post
office. But we didn't get any letters, because everyone had forgotten
about us. We never slept and because we didn't sleep, we didn't eat.
Now and then we sipped some water from a fountain. In the summer
it rained a lot, in the autumn we watched the birds heading south,
in winter it was cold and in spring the birds returned. We often wore
three pullovers at once and two pairs of trousers and two pairs of
shoes. We went from nowhere to nowhere getting to know all the street
names by heart. We went window shopping and thought about all the
things we didn't need.

Grandma lost her patience.
My brother stopped doing his homework and Mother did nothing to
help him.
Grandpa became forgetful.
But my father was very bored.
So ... we moved to the house with three phones.

The house with three phones

When we lived in the house with three phones we had a lot of fun. We each had our own floor and when we wanted to talk to each other, we picked up the phone. The house had a flat roof where we weren't supposed to go, but we did anyway. When we were bored we called each other by pretend names and told stories. Each phone had a different ring tone, though one didn't ring at all. But when you picked up the receiver you could hear people talking to each other softly in different languages. You had to be quiet, or they would stop speaking and hang up the phone.

Father lived on the fourth floor.
Grandpa lost another three teeth.
My sister spoke on the phone to two different people and Grandma said she had a secret admirer in Ankara.
But Mother had had enough of phones.
So ... we moved to the moon.

The moon

When we lived on the moon, it was quiet especially at night. In the evening the earth rose and in the morning it set. We were often freezing, and during the day we all had to wear sunglasses. We were surrounded by seas, but we couldn't swim in any of them. Sometimes ships flew over, and if they landed people wearing helmets would get out. We didn't know how to talk to them but we made them gifts of stones and dust, because that was all the moon had to offer. Perhaps that's why the people never came back.

Grandma said everything on the moon was only a quarter of its normal weight.
Father promised each of us a third of the world.
Mother slept half the time and my brother was short of breath for a whole day.
But Grandpa missed his girlfriends and his best mate.
So ... we moved to the cinema.

The cinema

When we lived in the cinema we always got up in the afternoon. Every evening we had lots of visitors. We ate only ice cream and popcorn and occasionally the peanuts we found between the seats. We drank coffee and coca-cola. Sometimes they showed films for grown-ups and our parents sent us outside. On Tuesdays we saw silent pictures and on Sunday afternoons we watched cartoons together. In the breaks you couldn't get into the toilets and after every performance we had to sweep up the rubbish.

Mother watched the same film 40 times.
Father didn't sit down with us until the adverts were over.
Grandpa understood only half of what the actors said and Grandma lost her favourite earring.
But my sister wanted to go to Casablanca.
So ... we moved into the rain.

The rain

When we lived in the rain, we couldn't see people's faces, because they were hidden under umbrellas and hoods. Our clothes clung to our bodies and we couldn't go inside, because outside was inside. Our hands and feet turned very pale and wrinkly and no one wanted to visit us any more or shake our hands. We didn't have to wash, but our hair and fingernails grew much quicker than usual.

My brother learnt the names of the four seasons.
Mother prayed to the Holy Trinity that the rain would stop.
Grandpa started seeing double.
But Grandma ran out of dry clothes.
So ... we moved to the white tent in the snow.

The white tent in the snow

When we lived in the white tent in the snow, everything was quiet and white – apart from the black night sky and our hands and feet turning blue. If you looked very closely, you could see there were lots of different types of snow flake. We counted almost 57 varieties before we stopped. We didn't need a fridge, but we had seven ovens: one each. There was more ice than we could possibly know what to do with, but we didn't eat it because it had no taste.

At zero degrees the snow was very soft.
At minus ten degrees it squeaked under our shoes.
At minus twenty it was as hard as ice, and at minus thirty our noses went numb and we felt stinging and pain in our feet.
But then it dropped to minus forty degrees.
So … we moved into the sea.

The sea

When we lived in the sea we tried talking to the fish but they never replied. When a storm raged, we swam close to the surface and saw the waves crash above us while we rocked up and down, and imagined we were flying. Sometimes when we played we turned upside down or rolled onto our sides until we forgot which way was up. Then we swam even deeper until we reached the bottom, where there were mussels and crabs and things that people had thrown into the water. Once we found a huge ship. In the galley the plates were still on the tables and in the pantry some fish had set up home in the cutlery drawers.

My brother saw four eels.
Grandpa did three somersaults.
Mother found two pearls.
But Father couldn't see anything under water.
So ... we moved into Uncle's hat.

Uncle's hat

When we lived in Uncle's hat we could hear everything he did and said. Not that he said or did much at all. He walked in the park and read his newspaper. He'd hang the hat on hat stands and we had to cling on tightly so we didn't fall off. Sometimes he'd forget his hat somewhere but he always found it again. In the shop where he bought his cheese he chatted to the assistant about France and the Pyrenees. When we peeped over the brim we saw his shoes far below. He polished them everyday so that you could see your face in them.

There were four times when Uncle said nothing at all.
Three times he forgot something important and couldn't remember it.
He met two women on a regular basis but kissed only one of them.
But his hat gave him a headache.
So ... I decided to move out and live on my own.

On my own

When I lived on my own I could do what I wanted. But because I had to do everything myself, I didn't have any free time. Once I'd finished washing my clothes it was already time to cook, and once I'd eaten I had to go to work to earn some money. I worked in a bakery and all day long I had to pack the warm loaves into paper bags and then into boxes. Every morning I watched television because I was so tired, and during the day I dreamed I was sitting in a bed on wheels, rolling down a hill. On Sundays I would take the tram through the city until it was dark. Then I'd go home and not turn the lights on but just keep humming along with the fridge, until it was time to go to work again.

I had four keys, but only three doors.
Twice it rained the whole night through and once it snowed in the middle of summer.
But then I got ill.
So I went looking for my family and found them living under a bridge.

A different bridge every night

When we lived under a different bridge every night, we saw many places and had plenty of time to think. Sometimes we had to walk for ages before we found a new bridge. Sometimes it smelt strange and the names of people we didn't know were written on the pillars. Because we had no money we asked passers-by for help. Some helped us, some didn't. When it snowed we looked for wood to make a fire. Then we took turns to watch the fire through the night so that it wouldn't die out. If you were all alone on fire duty, it was so quiet you could hear your stomach rumble.

Father led the way when we were tired.
My sister hopped on one leg in the morning.
Mother recited poetry she'd learnt when she was young.
Grandma had a cold that she couldn't shake off.
But one night Grandpa died while on fire duty.
So ... we moved into the dream.

The dream

When we lived in the dream small things were large and large things were small. Everything was on the move all the time and sometimes we saw elephants. It was more dark than light and often there were no colours. We couldn't smell anything, but we could see the smells. When we spoke, we couldn't hear each other, but we still knew what we were saying. We saw people we had never seen before. There were animals all around but hardly any plants. There was a forest but no trees. You could go down and down for ever without stopping, but never upwards. It was very hard to get anywhere – either that, or we'd be somewhere in a flash, because at times we could all fly.

We saw Grandpa four times, but he never saw us.
Once my brother was three metres tall, or even taller.
Father always wore his double-breasted suit.
And once Grandma woke up and couldn't go back to sleep.
But mother didn't recognise me any longer.
So ... we moved to our house.

Our house

Since we moved here, life has got so much better for us. We live in a big house that looks just like the houses either side of us. We don't have a garden, but there are flowers growing right behind our house. We hear the bells of three churches as they chime; sometimes we hear the wind and rain. We miss Grandpa a lot, but Uncle comes to visit every Monday. He tells us what he's been reading, or what the woman in the cheese shop had to say. Aunty recently wrote to say that she has taken up the violin again and asked if we could come to stay.

Now our house has four corners.
And our year has four seasons.
We moved here four years ago...
So ... this is where we'll live for a very, very long time.

Have a look at the resources section of our website where you will find free introductory booklets and audio downloads of our stories.

www.wingedchariot.com